빛과 소리는 하늘과 땅에서

Light and Sound
Twixt Sphere and Glebe

국립중앙도서관 출판예정도서목록(CIP)

빛과 소리는 하늘과 땅에서 : Light and Sound Twixt Sphere and
Glebe / 지은이 : 김종남. -- 서울 : 한누리미디어, 2018
    p. ;   cm

한영대역본임
ISBN 978-89-7969-787-2 03810 : ₩15000

한국 현대시 [韓國現代詩]

811.7-KDC6
895.715-DDC23   CIP2018041938

빛과 소리는 하늘과 땅에서
Light and Sound Twixt Sphere and Glebe

지은이 / 김종남   Poems of Jong-nam Kim
발행인 / 김영란   Publisher / Young-ran Kim
발행처 / **한누리미디어**   Publication / Hannurymedia
디자인 / 지선숙   Editing Design / Seon-sook Ji

08303, 서울시 구로구 구로중앙로18길   2F 40, Gurojoongangro18gil
40, 2층(구로동)   Gurogu Seoul, 08303
전화 / (02)379-4514, 379-4519   Telephone / 02) 379-4514, 379-4519
Fax / (02)379-4516   Fax / 02) 379-4516
E-mail/hannury2003@hanmail.net   E-mail / hannury2003@hanmail.net

신고번호 / 제 25100-2016-000025호   Report Number / 25100-2016-000025
신고연월일 / 2016. 4. 11   Report Date / 2016. 4. 11
등록일 / 1993. 11. 4   Date of Registration / 1993. 11. 4

초판발행일 / 2018년 12월 22일   The First Publication / 2018. 12. 22

ⓒ 2018 김종남 Printed in KOREA   ⓒ 2018 Jong-nam Kim Printed in KOREA

값 15,000원 $ 13,00

※잘못된 책은 바꿔드립니다.   *The damaged books are exchangeable.
※저자와의 협약으로 인지는 생략합니다.   *It stamps are omilted through agreement with the authe

ISBN 978-89-7969-787-2 03810   ISBN 978-89-7969-787-2 03810

Volume 7

빛과 소리는 하늘과 땅에서

Light and Sound
Twixt Sphere and Glebe

김 종 남
Jong-nam Kim

한누리 미디어

시인의 말

글로벌시대에 세계시인들과 서정적 교류는 인간의 정서를 평온케 하고 전 인류의 영원무궁을 가능하게 할 것이라는 소망으로 용기를 내어 정리하다 보니 일곱 번째 대역본(한영)으로 상재하게 되었다.

문학도 하나의 예술로 괴테가 말한 "예술 감각이 사라졌을 때 모든 예술작품은 사멸한다"는 말을 음미해 보면서 그의 문학세계에서 가장 중요한 관심사는 언제나 자연과 신이다. 그러나 그보다 더 중요한 모티브로서 그를 자극한 것은 인간적 열정에 대한 자기 확신이란 점이다.

자연과 역사는 시를 탄생시키는 요람이라 여겨 자연은 글의 내용과 방향을 정해 주고 역사는 써가야 할 길을 안내해 주는 것 같아 그 창작 활동은 고뇌와 산고의 삶이라 다짐해 본다.

8

일단 하나의 글이 세상에 발표된 후엔 작가의 것이 아닌 독자들의 몫이라, 제 역할을 다하기 위해선, 부담감 없이 읽고 나서, 이해하기 쉽고 정서가 넘쳐 흐르는 사상이 있어 누구에게나 깊은 감명과 감동을 줄 수 있어야 한다.

이 시집을 펴내면서, 초라한 내 안의 모습을 적나라하게 드러내 보이는 것 같아 부끄럽지만, 한편으로는 6집보다 7집이 더 나은 작품이란 평을 들었으면 좋겠다. 앞으로도 갈고 닦는 좋은 시를 쓰도록 노력하겠다.

2018년 12월 5일

김 종 남 올림

The Poet's Words

The lyrical interchange with the people of the world in the global age is encouraged by the desire to calm the emotions of humanity and enable the eternity of all mankind, I'm publishing my seventh collection of poems in parallel Korean and English.

Literature is also an art, as Goethe said, "When art senses disappear, all works of art die", His most important interests are Nature and God.

But what motivated him as a more important motive is self-confidence in human passion.

Nature and history are the cradles of birth of poetry. Nature defines the content and direction of writing, And history guides the way to write.

Therefore, it's considered that the creative activity is the life of agony and travail.

Once a single writing has been published in the world, it's a part of the reader, not the author.

After reading freely in order to fulfill all roles, it's an easy-to-understand and feeling idea. Everyone should be able to give a deep impression and emotion.

Publishing this poem, I'm abashed in my shabby inner appearance. But on the other hand I would like to hear the comment that the 7th collection is better than the 6th. I'll write a good poetry to polish.

December 5, 2018

Jong-nam Kim

11

| 차례 |

시인의 말 · 8
The Poet's Words · 10

1 계절 따라

020 계절 따라
According to the Season

022 낚시꾼의 단상
Fragmentary Thoughts on an Angler

024 눈과 눈의 스파클
The eyes Sparkling Twixt You and Me

026 디지털의 우상화
Idolization of Digital

028 사진 한 장
A Piece of Photo

030 어항 속 고기들
The Fishes of Aquarium

032 온 몸에 전율이
The whole Body Tremors

034 젊음의 꽃은 다시 피지 않는다 해도
Even though Flower of Youth doesn't bloom again

036 찌개를 끓이면
Boiling a Soup

038 청송으로 머물고 싶은 것을
Staying with a Green Pine

040 회한의 가책을 못 느낀 마법사
A Magician not to feel the Compunction of Remorse

12

작품해설 · 158
Explanation · 161

2 넝쿨장미

044   넝쿨장미
       Vine Roses

046   넝쿨장미의 춤가락
       Dancing Roses

048   동백꽃
       A Camellia

050   동백을 보면
       Seeing the Camellia

052   목련을 보면
       Seeing the Magnolia

054   벚꽃 일생
       Life of Cherry Blossoms

056   진달래의 추억
       Azalea's Memories

058   철쭉 송이송이
       A Bunch of Rhododendron

060   철쭉 향연
       Royal Azalea Banquet

062   피고 지는 꽃잎
       Blooming and falling Petals

13

3 들꽃을 바라보면

066 들꽃을 바라보면
Looking at the wild Flowers

068 바람과 파도
Wind and Waves

070 붉은 장미를 바라보면
Looking at red Roses

072 생각만 해도
Even though I think

074 여름 산행
Mountain-climbing in Summer

076 잡초를 보면
Seeing the Weeds

078 청산은
Green Mountain

080 초여름 소나무 숲
Pine Forest in early Summer

082 풀잎에 이슬
Dew Drops on the Blades

084 파도의 길
The Way of Waves

14

4 가을 나그네

088 가을 나그네
An Autumn Stranger

090 가을 산은
Fall Mountain

092 가을엔
Autumn

096 가을이 가는 소리
The sounds of Fall

098 가을 하늘 아래
Under the Autumn Sky

100 가을 흥취
Fall Interests

102 고향 그리워
A Nostalgic Hometown

104 구름의 방랑
The Wanderer of Clouds

106 국화꽃 단상
Chrysanthemum Fragmentary

108 추락하는 나뭇잎 보니
Seeing the falling Leaves

15

5 겨울 나뭇가지

112 겨울 나뭇가지
Winter Twigs

114 겨울 날 단상
Fragmentary of Winter Day

116 겨울 산 오르면
Climbing up Winter Mountain

118 겨울 향수
Winter Nostalgia

120 겨울 호숫가를 거닐면
Taking a stroll on the Lakeside in Winter

122 나목이여
Nude Trees

124 눈 내리는 속을
Through the falling Snow

126 설편의 일생
The Life of a Snow

128 설화를 바라보니
Looking at Snowflakes

130 함박눈이 펑펑 내려
Snow is coming down in large Flakes

16

6 나에게 주려는 선물

134 나에게 주려는 선물
A Gift meant for me

136 나팔수
Trumpeter

138 물결은
Waves

140 바람과 파도
Wind and Waves

142 수평선을 바라보면
Seeing the Horizon

144 어머님의 등은
My mother's Back

146 열심히 살 뿐
Living hard

148 자유자재의 나비
Butterflies of perfect Freedom

150 파도를 동경함은
Longing for the Waves

152 파도의 숨결
Breath of the Waves

156 해안선 따라
Along the Coastline

17

1

~~~~~~

계절 따라
According to the Season

계절 따라

봄이 오면 만물의 부활 속
그들의 꿈은 방실방실
피어날 것만 같아
마음의 설렘이 꽃잎 따라 서성서성

여름이 오면 초목이 무성해지는 활기참 속
그들의 푸른 꿈도 푸릇푸릇
번성蕃盛해질 것만 같아
마음의 희망들이 싱싱한 잎 따라 출렁출렁

가을이 오면 익어가는 열매의 금빛 속
그들의 굳은 꿈도 토실토실
결실을 맺을 것만 같아
가슴 속 부푼 기대감으로 바라보는 송이송이

겨울이 오면 그 하얀 눈보라 속
눈꽃 사이사이
공수래공수거의 영적 꿈길 따라
봄 사생화寫生畵를 바라보는 생각만 오락가락.

20

According to the Season

In the resurrection of all nature
　　When spring comes,
Their dreams seem to bloom beamingly
　　And the excitements of heart have lingered on the petals.

In the liveliness with lush vegetation
　　When summer comes, their blue dreams
Seem to flourish freshly
　　And the heart's hopes have surged with fresh leaves.

In the gold of the ripe fruits when autumn comes,
　　Their firm dreams seem to bear fruits plumply
And their bosoms have looked enviously at
　　A cluster of them with the puffy expectations.

In the white snowstorm when winter comes,
　　I only go back and forth with the thoughts
To look at the sketch of spring
　　Along the spiritual dream of "Come empty,
Return empty" among the snow flowers.

21

낚시꾼의 단상

고요한 호숫가
짝사랑의 고안孤雁
수면에 날아
부표浮標를 향한
애타는 연정

안으로 두려움과 불안으로 망설이고
밖엔 덫을 믿고 한가로운 기다림 속
속이려 함과 속아 주어야 하는 내적 전쟁

불현듯
찌가 흔들리다 솟아
잡아채는 조사釣絲의 긴장이
허무감으로 바뀔 때
눈과 귀는 바람에 위안 받고
울렁이는 가슴은 물결을 타고
한바탕 허공을 떠도는 소리 없는 한숨.

Fragmentary Thoughts on an Angler

A solitary wild goose of one-sided love
   On the shore of a serene lake flies
On the surface of the water.
   It's a tantalizing passion for the buoy.

Hesitating with fear and anxiety within the water
   And waiting leisurely to believe the trap outside,
They've an internal war to deceive
   And to be deceived between them.

When the tension of fish-line to snatch away
   From the water is changed
To feeling of futility through the buoy shakes
   And overtops suddenly,
His eyes and ears take comfort in wind.
   The palpitating heart rides on the wave
And at full blast, it's a silent sigh to drift
   In the air.

23

눈과 눈의 스파클

눈과 눈의 스파클
야릇한 감정의 질긴 끈이
뇌리를 포위
굴레의 노예가 된 몸

경모敬慕의 정을 누르지 못하고
내 마음은
송이 위로 인연의 파도

사귐과 믿음이란 관계 사이
수많은 세월을 엮어
이젠
난해한 순정의 터닝 포인트에
고뇌에 찬 퍼즐

못 견디게 순간순간마다
격정의 포로 된 자유로
뼛속까지 오싹하는
눈과 눈의 안주眼珠는
공간에서 총알이 부딪치듯 스파클.

24

The Eyes sparkling between You and Me

Through the eyes sparkling between you and me,
  The sturdy straps of odd emotion surround the brain
And have been a slave man.

Feeling an irresistible yearning for love and respect,
  My mind became a wave of destiny
O'er the clusters.

The years have gone by in the relation
  Between fellowship and faith.
For now, my mind has been the puzzle full of agony
  To the turning point of
The difficult pure-minded feeling.

At odd moments not to endure,
  The eyeballs of eyes and eyes to chill
To the marrow of my bones
  With the freedom enclaved from the passions
Are the sparkles like the bullets hit in space.

디지털의 우상화

이 세상
정보화 사회를 선도하는
터치 문화의 리더로
다양하고 놀라운 스피드의 세상

손가락 터치로
교제의 문자화
허와 실의 연합이
수많은 기능을 능가하는 요술妖術로
과학문명의 기도企圖가
일상생활의 창의성을 무디게 한 채

소음과 공중도덕의 공해를 망각한 듯
시청각이 부산하게 화면을 엄습하면
그 얼굴의 섬광閃光에 후리게 되어
스크린 뒤에
우상화의 대상으로
시간을 살인하는 숭배자들.

26

Idolization of Digital

This world is a diverse and amazing speed world
   As the leader of a touch culture
To guide an information-oriented society.

It makes a literation of fellowship
   With a touch of a finger.
The union of defect and substance performs
   Sleight-of-hand tricks
To surpass the magic number of functions.
   The scheme of scientific civilization has blunted
The creativity of everyday life.

It seemed to have forgotten the pollution
   Of noise and public morality.
If the visual and auditory senses make a surprise
   Suddenly attack on the screen,
We're bewitched by the flash of the face
   And the worshipers to murder times
Through the object of idolization
   On the snare of screen,

사진 한 장

사라진 모습들이
사진 한 장 속
회상되는 기억의 저 편
한 순간의 찰나에
핑 도는 마음의 한 조각

사진은 퇴색했지만
또렷이 드러나는
어머님에 그리움들이
내 마음 판 깊은 정원에
장미꽃 피어나듯
새록새록 솟는 감흥

미련과 아쉬움은
나의 생각 속
은은한 향기로만 맴돌아
어머님은 밖 화면으로
나는 안 추억의 세계로
이렇게 저렇게
오묘한 반추.

One Photo

The figures disappeared in a piece of photo
　Are dazzled on the far side
Of recalling memories.
　A piece of my mind is reeled
At that very moment.

It's faded,
　But the longings to my mother
To reveal clearly
　Are an inspiration to soar successively
As the roses bloom in my deep garden.

29

The attachments and regrets
　Have spun myself round
With only faint scent in my opinion.
　I've appreciated the profound rumination
Like this or that
　As my mother is out of the screen
And I'm in a world of memories inside.

어항 속 고기들

본향의 살기다툼을 타의로 탈출
한정된 투명한 공간에서
흐느적인 지느러미의 원동력으로
팔락거리는 아가미의 지칠 줄 모르는 기교技巧

유유창천悠悠蒼天을 나는 화살처럼
잠수부의 센 침하沈下나 숫구침같이
눈 부릅뜨고
자유자재 몸놀림하다
장벽에 짝사랑 퍼붓는
서글픈 사연에 선회旋回

진공 속에서
아무런 흔적도 남기지 않은 채
오직 순종과 인내의 몸부림치고
가깝고도 먼 나래짓이
나의 눈빛을 밀어내
내 마음은
부끄러움과 부러움에 서성이게 되는 단상斷想.

30

The Fishes of Aquarium

Escaping their competition for survival
   Of the homeland,
They exert their tireless technical skills
   Of the flapping gills like a sliding
Through the motive power of the fluttering fins
   In the limited clear space.

They make their glaring eyes and smart movements
   With perfect freedom like the arrows flying about
In the endless blue sky and a diver sinks robustly
   Or raises quickly
And then turn with the sad matters
   Of pouring an unrequited love on the barrier.

They challenge only the struggle
   Of obedience and perseverance
Without leaving any traces in the vacuum.
   Their near and far flaps of the wings push out
The glitter of my eyes.
   Hereby, my heart has felt my fragmentary thoughts
That come to shame and envy.

온몸에 전율이

차도 따라 인도를 걷노라면
빙판길보다
싸늘한 총알처럼 쾌주하는
자동차의 소음에
아찔한 두려움이

보도의 좁은 길 걷노라면
내뿜는 매연공해보다
붐비는 군중 속
끌려가는 강아지의 무거운 걸음과
요란한 소리들로
역겨운 냉가슴이

십자로에 이를 때면
살아있는 듯한 CCTV는
독취禿鷲의 눈동자처럼
내 속을 들여다보는 것 같아
온몸에 전율이.

32

The whole Body Tremors

Walking the foot path along the driveway,
    I've felt the giddy fear in the noise of the car
That runs more like a chill bullet than an icy roads.

Walking the narrow foot path,
    My heart is disgusted at the heavy pace
Of the puppies to be pulled along by force
    Into the bustling crowd and the loud sounds
Than a smoke pollution.

Reaching the crossroads,
    I've felt my whole body tremor
As the lifelike CCTV looks into my heart
    Like the pupils of an eagle.

젊음의 꽃은 다시 피지 않는다 해도

세월이 흐름에 따라
잠시 잠깐 눈 감아 보면
젊은 날의 영롱한 사운드는
골수의 창문을 노크하고

시간을 다투어 일하여 싸웠음에도
그 시절은 감미롭고
땀과 눈물 닦던
추억의 손수건은 접어졌고

유년기는 아리송한 눈
청년기엔 열정의 눈빛
반세기도 지난 지금엔
하얀 머리카락 만지작거리며
거울 앞에 과거 행위에 대한
통한의 깃발을 응시하게 되고

젊음의 봄은 다시 오지 않는다 해도
영원을 사모하는 소망 하나 바라보며
현재의 시간에 맞서
일하고 노래하리.

Even though Flower of Youth doesn't bloom again

If my eyes are shut a little while
   In the course of years,
The serene voices of my young days have knocked
   The windows of the bone marrow.

Working and struggling against times,
   I've experienced a sweet taste at that time
And the handkerchiefs of memories to wash off
   Sweats and tears were folded.

Childhood has overflowed with ghostly eyes
   And youth with passional eyes.
It's also the last half-century now.
   Fingering my white hair,
I've gazed at the flag of keen regret for past deeds
   In front of mirror.

Even if spring of youth doesn't come back again.
   Looking at one yearning for eternity,
I want to work and sing against present time.

찌개를 끓이면

냉장고의 종류대로 시체들
오만 무례를 범하면서까지
허기짐 달래기 위해
갈등과 결단을 모아
냄비에 담기면
빗발치듯 불꽃 위
뒤엉킨 시체는 꽃을 엮어 화환을 만들듯
보글보글

용암에 분출물처럼
벌겋게 끓는 찌개는
넘치기도 하고 졸아지기도 하여
향과 영양소로
지글지글

식탁으로 옮겨
뚜껑이 열릴 때까지도
여전히 솟는 향취는
격자格子 무늬 감칠맛으로
모락모락.

36

Boiling a Soup

Pulling the carcasses according to their kinds
    Out of a refrigerator,
Collecting the conflicts and resolutions
    And Putting them in the pot to appease my hunger
As I commit the arrogant and impertinent attitude,
    The entangled carcasses seem to bubble like twisting
Flowers into a wreath on the shower of sparks.

The stew soup to be boiled with a florid red
    As an extravasate of lava is overflowed
And boiled down.
    I feel a good appetite to be boiled
By flavor and nutrients with a sizzling sound.

It moves to the table and sends forth fragrance
    To gush up still and more
Even when the lid is opened.
    I'm nice to the palate of lattice figure
To puff up with hot steam.

청송으로 머물고 싶은 것을

양심의 거울 앞에 서면
그지없는 부끄러움에
고개 들지 못한 육신

흙으로 만든 것이 생령이 된 인생
빈손으로 왔기에 조금씩 비워 보지만
세월 따라
영육간 연합에 한 몸은
생의 애착에 노예근성의 존재

지난 젊음의 낭만은
세파世波에 숨겨진 그 무엇을 구하기 위해
망망대해 항해로 지친 풀잎 같은 헛된 망상
이제는
한 줄기 바람이 인사만 해도
외로운 구름 같은 나그네
부질없는 낙엽으로 구르는 초로草露
세상 속 쓸쓸한 영혼의 눈빛 안고
한갓 청송으로 머물고 싶은 것을.

38

Staying with a Green Pine

Standing in front of a mirror of conscience,
　I'm a flesh who can't hold up my head
For endless shame.

The man is formed from the dust of the ground
　And becomes a living being.
Life comes with empty hands,
　And it empties little by little.
But with the years,
　One body of union twixt spirit and body
Is the being of slavery in the attachment of life.

The romance of last youth to get something hidden
　In the storms of life was a meaningless phantasm
Like the leaf to be tired from the voyage
　Of boundless ocean.
Now, even if a streak of wind is greeted,
　I'm a dew drop on a grass blade to be tumbled
Of meaningless leaves as a lonely cloudy stranger.
　Embracing the color of sad soul's eyes of the world,
I just want to stay with the green pine.

회한悔恨의 가책을 못 느낀 마법사魔法師

바람은
무형과 무색의 형체로
세상 요리조리 구석구석 넘나드는
자유로운 무법자無法者

스스로 존재한 것처럼
그대의 발길이 닿으면
생사生死의 갈림길에
혁명을 꿈꾸는 절대 권위자權威者

속은 드러내지 않은 채
변화무쌍變化無雙한 파워에
흔적 없이 지나는 그대의 입김은
동식물의 쾌감과 좌절을 좌우지하는
변덕스러운 요술객妖術客

우주공간 연습 없는 무언극에
그대의 날갯짓은
온갖것 어루만지고도
멈추지 못한 채
회한의 가책을 모르는 마법사魔法師.

40

A Magician not to feel the Compunction of Remorse

The wind is a colorless and intangible form.
    It's a free outlaw who crosses the world
Here and there and all over.

As a present for thyself,
    If thy feet touch, thou art an absolute authority
Who expects a revolution at the crossroads of life
    And death.

As it doesn't expose the inner.
    Thy breath to pass without a trace
In the kaleidoscope of power is a chopping conjurer
    To command the pleasure and frustration
Of animals and plants.

Thy wings have looked askance at all kinds of things
    Through the pantomime not to have a rehearsal
In outer space.
    But as it isn't stopped, a magician not to feel
The compunction of remorse.

2

넝쿨장미
Vine Roses

넝쿨장미

온몸이 가시 갑주甲胄로
은은한 열정적 사기士氣는
초병哨兵의 불타는 눈빛처럼
은밀히 피어나는 송이송이

절벽에 온몸을 밀착한 채
은혜의 햇빛과 연합
화려한 꽃잎을 만들어내는
창조자의 숨결을 풍기는 상냥한 미소

나비의 입술은 숨바꼭질로
아름다운 사색을 승화시키고
벌들의 편대는 윙윙 곡예사로
꽃밥 키스는 꽃맺이를 바라는 큰 기쁨

바람결에 속살까지 보이는 꽃무늬에
눈길 따라 수지手指 가까이 하니
날카로운 가시는 중얼거리는 억양인 양
아득한 미의 여운은 멀리서 바라봄이
진리라 하네.

44

Vine Roses

As the whole body is a thorny amor,
  The latent enthusiastic fraud is a cluster
Of vine roses that flourishes in private
  Like the burning eyes of sentinel.

Adhering closely to the cliff, they've showed me
  An amiable smile that gives the creator's breath
To produce gorgeous petals in combination with
  The sunshine of grace.

The lips of butterflies sublimate
  The beautiful meditation in hide-and seek
And the bees' formation is a great pleasure
  For the kiss of anther to desire the newborn fruit
As a humming acrobat.

The aftereffect of distant beauty is said to be true
  To look up from distance
As the sharp thorns become a murmurous tone,
  Closing my fingers within my eyes
To the flower pattern to be seen the inside flesh
  In the wind.

45

넝쿨장미의 춤가락

햇살 품어
신묘神妙한 생명체의 율동
순연純然한 애착의 착색着色은
연분홍 진분홍 다홍색으로
환열歡悅에 찬 열정의 입술들

바람에 나부끼는
요염한 자태의 외침이
펄쩍 날 듯
지천至賤으로 꽃잎 열어
단아端雅한 정열적 제스처

매혹적인 핏빛 흐드러지게
곡선미의 몸뚱이 휘감아
뭉클뭉클 피어오르는 불꽃 무리처럼
요리조리 춤가락
내 안구眼球도 그 댄서들과 파트너.

Dancing Roses

They show a wonderful creature's rhythm
    In the sunshine.
The colorations of pure affection are passionate lips
    In an ecstasy of joy with light, deep pink
And crimson.

The screams of a charming figure in the wind
    Open the petals humbly as if they flew suddenly.
They're a pure passionate gesture.

The curvy bodies tangled with vine roses
    In the fetching bloody color of splendor
Like a crowd of flaming fire to rise into the air
    Are a dancing act this way and that.
My eyeballs to see the scene are a partner
    With the dancers.

47

동백꽃

설한풍에
인고의 세월 지킨 품위
부푼 젖가슴 찢은 얼이
화사한 웃음꽃 날갯짓

하늘과 땅 사이
분홍 꿈 가슴 문 여니
수줍게 내미는 보석 같은 얼굴에
초롱초롱한 미소는
정한情恨과 함께 환상의 아름다움

터질 듯 눈부신 네 모습은
환희의 몸부림으로
서로를 흐뭇하게 하여
내 사악한 마음은
핏빛 그리운 연정으로
추억과 망각의 속삭임을
내 가슴 판에 새기고 싶구나.

48

A Camellia

They maintain the dignity to be endured
    The stoic years of bitter cold snowfall and wind.
The torn spirit with bloated chest spreads
    A bright laughing wing.

Opening the heart of the pink dream in the world,
    Thy clear and bright smile on the face like a gem
Of the shy expression is the beauty of fantasy
    With love and regret.

Thy brilliant appearance to be burst
    Makes happiness with one another
With the struggle of joy.
    My wicked heart wants to engrave the whispers
Of memories and forgetfulness in my chest board
    Through the burning passion of blood long.

49

동백을 보면

초록 치맛자락에 포로된 알몸
붉은 입술엔 난황卵黃 같은 미소
멀리서 바라보는 안타까움만
올랑 촐랑

세상 속 십자가에
피맺힌 안주眼珠를 바라보듯
내 양심의 넋은
혈관을 촐랑 출렁

밤하늘에 별빛처럼 망각되지 못한 채
밤이슬과 연합해 내 마음 씻듯
참았던 눈물처럼
갈쌍 글썽

평강이 없는 가지 끝 등불 켜 들고
향수를 달래듯 노래 부르니
정념에 붉은 가슴이 미어지듯
올랑 울렁.

Seeing the Camellia

They're the naked body captured in the green skirt
    And their red lips have a smile like a yolk.
The tedium of looking from afar is slapping
    Hither and thither.

Looking at the blood-stained eyeballs
    On the cross in the world,
My soul of conscience behaves frivolously
    And laps about the blood vessel.

Without being forgotten like starlight
    In the night sky,
My pent-up tears are about to cry
    And filled with tears
As they wash my mind with the union
    Of the dew at night.

Lighting up a lamp at the end of a branch
    With no peace and singing with a charming voice
As if to comfort a warm nostalgia,
    My red heart of feeling and thought palpitates
And goes pitapat heart-rendingly.

목련을 보면

이른 봄 미풍에 실려
풍기는 기운에
겉살 적나라하게 찢고
순결한 미소의 요란한 잔치

새 봄 바람결에
순백의 날개는
사악한 세상을 환하게 하고
파란 겹겹 호위병 은혜로
그 봉오리 상위 석에 올려
비천飛天의 영혼 같은 침향沈香의 빛

유행도 모르는 채
청순한 백조의 날갯짓
제멋대로 내려앉는 호들갑을 보노라면
모든 것이 헛되고 헛되어
더 가야 할 내 여정에
목적 없이 슬픈 왈츠*의 선율이 귓전을 때려
흔들리는 나의 스텝.

*작곡 : 시벨리우스(1865~1957, 핀란드 사람)
*원명 : Valse Triste
*연대 : 1903
*내용 : 장중한 어조의 무곡

52

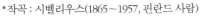

Seeing the Magnolia

In the aura to float on the breeze
   In the early spring,
They tear off the bare skin without reserve
   And have a festive feast of pure smile.

The pure white wings in the wind of new spring
   Make a wicked world with brightness
And put it on top of the bud with the grace
   Of blue guard in many folds.
And then they show the aloes' color
   Like the spirit of nymph.

Without knowing the fashion,
   When I see the flippantness
For the pure swan wings to come down arbitrarily,
   Everything is meaningless and utterly meaningless.
The melody of the sad waltz* without purpose
   Strikes my ears and my steps are swayed
On my journey to go more.

*Composer : Jan Sibelius(1865~1957, Finlander)
Original Name : Valse Triste
Years : 1903
Contents : Dancing and music in a solemn tone.

벚꽃 일생

부동자세의 대지에
실바람 일어
그 화려한 왈츠에
온몸 율동으로 봄 축제

연주자나 지휘자도 없이
널 위해
깊은 가슴 열어
하얀 드레스 찢으면서까지
함박눈 펄펄 내리는 향연饗宴

목화송이 활짝 피어
흰 종이쪽처럼 낙화로 흩어져
새 천지를 여니
온 가슴 두근거리게 하는 흔회欣懷

그들은 신부의 면사포로
바람 타고 왔다가
흰 수의壽衣로 사라지는
너무나 짧은 일생.

Life of Cherry Blossoms

A light breeze is getting up on the earth
    In an immobile posture.
The festival of spring is in full swing
    With the rhythm of the gorgeous waltz.

They open their deep heart for someone
    Without a performer or conductor.
I see the banquet for the great snowflakes
    To come down in a whirl
Till the white dresses tear.

They bloom in all their glory like the cotton balls
    And are strewn with fallen petals
As a piece of white papers.
    Opening the new world,
I feel the joy with my heart throbbing.

They're but a short life
    That they come by the wind with their bride veil
And disappear to be shrouded in the white.

진달래의 추억

바람 끝이 아직은 차가운데
가려진 알몸의 고운 살결은
수줍은 처녀의 볼을 보여주는 듯

잊고 살아온 지난 일들의 회상 속
첫사랑 화사한 미소를
들추어내는 부끄러운 속내

너무나도 아름다움에
만지고 꺾으려 했던 일
생각만 해도 안타까움에
마음이 저려

잊지 못할 고향 그 동산에
그대의 숨결인 양
핑크빛 토해내는
애절한 진달래 추억의 페이지.

Azalea's Memories

The end of the wind is still cold.
I've the feeling for the fine skin
On the naked body to be hidden
To show the cheeks of the shy virginity.

It seems to look at the shy insides
That retrace the bright smile of my first love
In the reminiscence of past things
That have been forgotten.

My heart is numbed in a fret
Even though I think about what I tried to touch
And break with so much beauty.

That's a page of memory of a sad azalea
To express the pink
As if I saw your breath
To the unforgettable garden.

철쭉 송이송이

능선 따라
한들 흔들 스윙에
울컥 토해 놓는 열정의 봄 찬미

겨울 잠 깨어나
피처럼 붉은 송이
가지마다 핏발 매달릴 때
푸른 잎 장병들 사이사이
부푼 꽃봉오리같이 솟구치면
칼바람에 피 흘리듯
요원지화燎原之火처럼 번지는
화들짝 활달한 웃음

살랑 설렁 꽃잎마다
반추의 몸부림이
햇살과 키스하면
만발한 봉오리는 하늘 향해
나팔을 불 듯
미소의 매력.

A Bunch of Rhododendron

It's the spring feast of passion to vomit out
   In the swing wavering along the ridge.

When the winter sleep wakes up,
   The blood-red bunches hang on every branch
And they raise quickly as a fat bud
   Among the green leaves soldiers,
It's an open laughing with slush
   To spread like wildfire as bleeding
In a cutting wind.

If the writhing of rumination on each petal
   With a rustle kisses the sunshine,
It's the sapidity of smile
   As if the blossoming bud blows the trumpet
Toward the sky.

59

철쭉 향연

공원 길
담장 길에
지천으로 유유상종
하늘 향해 뽐내는 군상

봄볕에
새 힘 기르는
위풍당당한 선구자

자연의 섭리에
신선한 잎 날개를 펴
음보音譜는 보이지 않은 채
새 희망의 잔치를 펼치는
봄 메아리 향연

그들의 빨간 입술들은
밤마다 빛나는 별들의 영원을 사모하여
만발한 봉오리는 그들을 닮아
흐드러지게 핀
늦봄 꽃잎 반향反響의 불길로 활활.

60

Royal Azalea Banquet

On a park or fence road,
  It appears as a brave crowd towards sky
Through birds of a feather flock together
  In superabundance.

It's an awe-inspiring pioneer
  Of new power-boosting in the spring scenery.

They spread their fresh leaf wings
  To the providence of nature.
It's opened out a banquet of spring echoes
  To unfold a new hopeful feast
As the musical note isn't visible.

Their red lips long for the eternity of the stars
  That shine every night
And the clusters burst into flames of petals' echoes
  To come out splendidly in late spring
That resemble them.

61

피고 지는 꽃잎

맑은 공기에 청아한 이슬 머금고
앞 다투어 피어난 꽃송이
은은한 향내로
이 세상을 요리할 때
사람들은 흥에 겨워 얼싸안아 키스하여
오감의 맛 만끽하고

시간에 쫓겨
그 화려했던 꽃잎
생기를 잃고 시들어
여생의 무대 커튼이 내려질 땐
그 어떤 동정심의 눈빛마저도 사라져
처량한 세상의 어두운 길 헤매며

꽃잎의 추락처럼
나 또한
세월과 함께 늙고 죽어가는 것도 서러운데
서로의 사귐에서 소외되고 어두운 길 걷노라면
그 외로움과 두려움을
어떻게 하소연하고 해소할 거나?

62

Blooming and Falling Petals

Having neat dew in clear air,
　　When the blossoms bloomed competitively
Cook the world with a subtle scents,
　　People are so excited that they embrace and kiss
And enjoy the taste of five senses.

The gorgeous petals that were chased by time
　　Lose their vitality and fade away.
As the stage curtain of the rest of their life
　　Falls down,
Even though the expression of their sympathy
　　Disappears,
They wander the dark roads of the world.

Like the fall of a petal,
　　Even as I'm old and feel sad to die with time,
If I'm cut off from the other members of my friends
　　And walk in the dark roads,
How do I complain and resolve to that loneliness
　　And fear?

63

3

들꽃을 바라보면
Looking at the wild Flowers

들꽃을 바라보면

햇빛 은혜로
여린 몸 율동하며
아름답게 반짝이는
해맑은 얼굴 얼굴들

파란 물결로 바람 불면
부드러운 살결 상하지 않고
쓰러졌다 다시 일어서는
오뚝이 기백이 부러워지고

거무스름한 체격과 단순한 동작으로
침묵의 눈빛 싸움하면서도
속삭이며 키재기하고
햇살과 공기 함께
서로 화응和應하는 모습을 응시하면
모질고 악착스럽게 피어나는
화려한 겸손의 참 얼굴들.

66

Looking at the wild Flowers

Their tender bodies play in rhythm
   And show the fair-skinned face and faces
To sparkle beautifully with sunshine grace.

When the wind blows with blue waves,
   It's the envy of the forceful spirit of tumbler
To fall down and get up again
   As the soft fair skins aren't hurt.

Fighting silently in their eyes
   With a darkish physique and simple action,
They whisper and measure their height.
   Gazing at the figure to harmonize each other
With sunshine and air,
   I see the true faces of brilliant humility
That begin to bloom cruelly and persistently.

바람과 파도

바람의 연주 따라
파도는 희고 푸른 드레스 댄스
찬란하게 갈라진 가슴과
시원하게 웃는 입술은
막막한 바다 위 환상적 예술

도둑같이 오가는 해락偕樂에
그토록 곡선미 넘치는 정열
잠들지 못한 맨몸으로
연신 부서지면서 외로움을 달래는 아우성

바람은
얼굴 빛깔도 없는 자유 분망한 자로
바다 속까지 헤집다
구만리장천九萬里長天에 잠들고
파도는
아무런 의미도 없이
하얀 거품 하나로 울음의 희락喜樂

난
그들의 연합전선에 석양에 사냥꾼.

| 김종남 제7시집 | 빛과 소리는 하늘과 땅에서

Wind and Waves

The waves dance in the white and blue dress
    Along the performance of the wind.
The chest chapped splendidly
    And coolly smiling lips are fantastic art
O'er the vast ocean.

It's such a curvy passion in enjoying together
    That comes and goes as thieves
And a shout that keeps loneliness
    By breaking down in a naked body
Not to be fallen asleep.

The wind is a free and busy man
    With no face and no color,
And he drifts into the sea and falls asleep
    In the boundless sky.
The wave shows me the pleasure of crying
    With one white foam without any meaning.

I'm a hunter in the sunset on their united front.

붉은 장미를 바라보면

줄기차게
푸른 하늘 사모하는 마음 문 열어
정다운 봉오리마다
붉은 입술의 향기가
바람 타고 흐를 때
자연의 영광 앞에
전원 교향곡을 감상한 듯

햇살과 바람을 만나
자유롭게 열애하고
나비나 꿀벌을 만나면
아무런 대가성도 없이
화분花粉을 선물하고

보면 만지고 싶고
만지면 꺾고 싶은
순간적 충동을 억누르고
바라만 볼 수밖에 없어
아름다움은 멀리서 바라봄이
영원한 기쁨의 참 진리인 것을.

70

Looking at Red Roses

They open the door of their hearts
  Of longing for blue sky with perseverance.
Every good bud,
  When the fragrance of red lips flows in the wind,
I enjoy the pastoral symphony
  In front of the glory of nature.

They meet with sunshine and wind
  And love fervently in freedom.
Meeting the butterflies and bees,
  They give the pollen as a present
Without any pricing.

Seeing the red roses, I want to touch them.
  And touching them, break them.
But I have to press down the impulse
  And no choice besides being forced
To see them.
  It's the truth of eternal joy
For the beauty to look at from afar.

생각만 해도

생각만 해도
땀방울이 흘러내릴 듯 한여름 밤
별들의 다정한 속삭임을 바라보다 잠들면
여동생과 멍석 위에서 숯불 다리미질하면서
피곤한 하루의 주름살을 펴시던 엄마

생각만 해도
보릿고개 땐
묽은 죽으로 자식들 눈빛 훔쳐
안쓰러워하시던 그 열정으로
삼베이불 덮어 주시던 그대

생각만 해도
두근거려지는 심장의 고동
밤 깊어 모깃불도 꺼져 삼경으로 달리면
난 스스로 잠들다 삶의 노크에 눈 떠 보니
앉은 채로 꼬박 지샌 어머니
지금은 추억의 회초리
문득문득 내 가슴을 두드리네.

Even though I think

In midsummer night that seems to be sweated
  Even though I think,
When I look at the affectionate whispers of stars
  And fall asleep, you're my mother to spread wrinkles
Of a tired day while ironing the charcoal
  On a straw mat with my younger sister.

Overcoming the spring famine even though I think,
  You're my mother to cover the bed-clothes of hemp
With the passion to steal the eyes of her children
  And feel sorry through the water gruel.

73

In the heartbeat to be throbbed even though I think,
  When the smoke to drive away mosquitoes
Goes out and runs at the dead night,
  You're my mother to sit nodding
And stay up all night for me to fall asleep on my own
  And wake up to the knock of life.
Now that has knocked my heart out
  As the whips of memories.

여름 산행

침묵 속
수목이 목례하는 사이사이 길
제자리 지키는 엄숙한 기암절벽
상망喪亡된 자아를 찾기 위한
연단의 한 걸음 한 걸음

신선한 공기에 햇빛도 충만
초록빛 윙크는 내 혼을 불러
세상의 덧없음 사색으로 날리고
순응하는 자연의 법칙 배우라 하고

가쁜 호흡 사냥개처럼 달리다 멈추면
초목의 반짝임과 산새소리 대합창에
순간마다 휘감기는 갈등은
피로한 갈증과 연상聯想되어
내 영혼 넉넉한 청산과 함께
높고 낮음 서로 비교하지 않는
설레는 정서 안고
하산해야 하는 마음 아쉬워.

74

Mountain-climbing in Summer

I go up step by step for the discipline
 To find a lost myself
Along the paths among the trees exchange nods
 And solemn rocky cliff that keeps the proper place
In silence.

The fresh air is filled with the sunlight,
 So the green wink calls my soul out
And the vanity of worldly things is blown
 By the speculation
And says to learn the law of conforming nature.

When my labored breathing stops running like a hound,
 My mind to go down is a felt want
As holding the green wind emotion
 That my spirit doesn't compare to each other
At high and low with the abundant green mountain
 For the conflicts happening every moment
To be reminded of tired thirst
 Through the great chorus of vegetation twinkling
And mountain birds' sounds.

잡초를 보면

온 들판에 아름다운 얼굴들
햇살의 기상나팔에
일제히 일어서는 생명력의 코러스
나의 시청을 유혹하여
심장이 울렁울렁
신명申明에 황홀감을

새벽이슬로 샤워하고
살려는 의욕이
짓밟히고 학대당해도
무성하고 씩씩한 기상을 보이며

바람결에 흔들리는 춤가락은
방치된 존재의 한恨을 바라보는 즐거움인데
날마다 순간마다
쓸쓸한 삶이
허무로 징징거리고 있네.

76

Seeing the Weeds

The beautiful faces in the whole field
　Are a grand chorus of vitality
To arise all at once on the reveille of the sun.
　Tempting my sight and hearing,
I'm enraptured o'er expressing thoughts
　As my heart goes pit-a-pat

They take a shower with dawn dew.
　The desire to live shows the lush
And fervent spirit
　Even if it's trampled and abused.

77

Dancing rocking in the wind is a pleasure
　For me to look at a bitter feeling
Of neglected beings.
　But, my lonely life is vain and crying out
Every day and moment.

청산은

안개에 싸인 산들이 걷히면
하늘과 땅 사이 울려 퍼지는
악보 없는 서곡의 대합창

낮이면 산자락 따라
활짝 돋아난 새싹들
밤이면 별들이 속삭이는
아름다운 정경 속
푸른 하늘과 산새소리에
눈물이 그리워지는 감동의 한 아름

왔던 길 회고하니
기암괴석 꽃이 핀 숲과 도란거리는 계곡물
그리고 밝은 햇살로 내 영육을 평화롭게 하는
어머님 품안 같은 곳

내 삶의 카타르시스는
청산의 녹색 물결과 하나 되어
하늘과 산봉우리 사이
사색의 날개를 펴리.

78

Green Mountains

When the mountains veiled in mist clear off,
   It's a great chorus of overture
Without musical note that resonated
   Twixt sphere and glebe.

There are young shoots now in full flush
   Along the hem of mountain during the daytime
And is an armful excitement
   For me to be yearned after the tears
Through the blue wind and mountain birds' sounds
   In the beautiful scenery
Where the stars whisper at night.

Recollecting the way I came,
   I feel the flowering forest and vale water to murmur
Of fantastic rocks and stones
   And like the bosom of my mother
Who makes my body and soul peaceful
   With soft and sunshine.

My catharsis of life is united with the green wave
   Of green mountain
And spreads the wings of speculation
   Twixt heaven and mountain peak.

초여름 소나무 숲

성큼 다가온 초여름
푸르스름한 파도에
싱그러운 잎들의 경쟁

따가운 햇살이 산야를 기웃대면
소나무 숲은 녹색의 환희
새 솔잎은
호리호리한 몸매로
죄 없이 산다는 것을 보이면서
춤추고 노래하는 생각조차도 사치라 여겨
푸른 교만의 고개 떨군 채
희로를 모르는 바위 같은 자로

봄과 이별하는 아쉬움이
꽃 찾는 벌이나 나비에 비하리오만은
나는
허공을 휘젓는 가지의 신비로움을 보니
시린 마음만을 달래는 그리움과 허전함.

80

Pine Forest in early Summer

Competition of flesh leaves is in full swing
   On a bluish wave approaching in a stride.

When the sunlight looks in on the fields
   And mountains,
The pine forest is a green joy.
   The new pine leaves seem to live without sin
With a slender figure.
   Even the thought of dancing and singing
Seems to be a luxury.
   Hanging down their heads of blue pride,
They're like rocky people who don't know
   Feeling of joy and anger.

The felt want to separate from spring
   Can't be compared to bees and butterflies
Looking for flowers.
   Seeing the mysteriousness of the branch
To stir up the air, I feel the yearning and emptiness
   Soothing my cold heart.

81

풀잎에 이슬

풀잎에 갈증 방울방울
햇살과 함께 크리스털 반짝반짝
현악의 선상에 굴러
어슴푸레하게 선율의 눈물방울

풍진 세상 속
새록새록 맺히는
진주 같은 물방울은
햇빛 은혜로 유아독존

창조의 손길이
풀잎 몸 스쳐
맑은 이슬 눈 잎사귀로
서로에게 힘이 되어주는
찬란한 삼라만상

떨어지지 않으려는 님프같이 송알송알
풀잎 끝자락에 그렁그렁 눈물로 소멸

82

윤회의 삶을 너로 인해 알겠네.

Dew Drops on the Blades

There are in drops of thirst in grass leaves
   And glittering crystals with sunshine.
They're the tear drops of melody in a faint
   Which roll on the strings of string music.

In troubles of the world,
   The pearl-like droplets forming
In succession
   Are self-conceited status with the grace
Of sunlight.

The hands of creation touch grass-leaf bodies.
   The bright universe is unfolded
That gives strength to each other
   With leaves of clear eyes of dew.

In beads like a nymph that doesn't want to fall,
   They've died out tearfully
At the end of the blades.

I know the life of transmigration owing to you.

83

파도의 길

여명의 안개 속 은빛 시린 물결이
꿈틀거리며 일어서는 워밍업으로
고요를 흔들어
원근遠近에 빠른 율동으로
연주하듯 오락가락

햇빛 터치로
벌거벗으면서까지 낮은 자세로
지칠 줄 모르는 인고의 몸부림이
흰 포말의 스토리만 남긴 채
물보라 향연에 어울린 왈츠

모양이나 그림자도 없는 몸이
한 자리 머물지 못해
심연으로의 치달음으로
숙덕숙덕 손짓하는 해초와 함께
세월을 낚는 자적自適에
가야 하는 파도의 길.

84

The Way of Wave

In the fog of the dawn,
  Shaking calm through the warming-up
For the silvery ripples to wriggle and rise,
  They come and go far and near
As they play in quick rhythm.

As the struggle of the endurance
  Which doesn't tire in a low posture
Until he's naked with the touch of sunlight
  Has left only the story of white bubble,
It's a waltz that suits the feast of spray.

As the body without shape or shadow can't stay
  In one place,
It's the way of wave to go
  Through the self-satisfaction of catching the years
With the seaweed that is beckoning
  With whisper secrets
Into the running up to the abyss.

4

가을 나그네
An Autumn Stranger

가을 나그네

모진 풍파 헤쳐 온 삶
세월의 돛단배 타고
앞뒤 풍경화를
마음 판에 그리며
팔십 산정에서
황혼의 놀을 바라보는 존재

막연한 그리움에
보람된 삶의 오직 한 길
끝닿을 곳 몰라
허탈감 속 두 눈이 지친 외로움에도
가을 나그네는 끝없이 도전하는 존재

채우고 채워도 채워지지 않는 욕망을 안고
세월 따라
어둠이 내리는 가을 녘
갈바람에 무거운 발길은
철새처럼 쓸쓸한 마음으로
낙엽을 밟고 산책을 해야 하는 존재.

An Autumn Stranger

Riding a sailboat o'er time
　　And engraving front and back landscape paintings
On the tablet of heart
　　Through my life to be emerged
From the contemptible storm,
　　I'm looking at the twilight glow
From the top of a mountain of the eighty.

I don't know where I end up in only one way
　　Of the worth life of vague longing.
Even though the eyes are tired of loneliness
　　In the depressed feeling, I'm endless challenges.

Holding the unfulfilled desire not to be filled
　　Though I fill and fill,
My heavy footsteps in the west winds
　　Of the fall evening of darkness by years
Are in the existence to take a walk
　　O'er the fallen leaves in a lonely mind
Like a migratory bird.

89

가을 산은

가을하늘 은혜로운 미소에
위풍당당 산봉우리는
저 지평선 상 눈부신 빛
현이 되어 울려 퍼지고
칠보단장의 처녀처럼
엄숙 단정한 그대

산정 언저리 뭉게구름 드레스는
웨딩마치로 지나가고
돌아올 수 없는
한 시즌의 끝자락에
오채영롱의 단풍으로
겨울을 재촉하는 그대

가을 산은
시원한 바람결에 청향이 발산하고
서서히 추락의 이별에 줄기와 잎새의 춤가락은
내 마음의 발걸음을 잠시 멈추게 하고
인간사회 소음을 피해
겨울 하얀 길로
손짓하듯 부르는 그대.

Autumn Mountain

The commanding mountain peaks in the graceful smile
    Of the autumn sky resonate with the strings
In accordance with the dazzling light on that horizon.
    You're solemn and tidy
Like a beautifully dressed-up virgin
    With the seven treasures.

The cumulous cloud dress on the summit bounds
    Of the mountain passes by a wedding march.
You're a figure who urges the winter
    With the maple leaves of brilliance
In all the five colors
    At the end of a season that can't come back.

The autumn mountain spreads out the perfume
    In the cool wind.
The dancing rhythm of branches and leaves
    In the slowly falling farewell seems to stop
My steps on my mind
    And avoid the human society noise.
You beckon with the hands in the white road
    Of winter.

91

가을엔

가을엔
산들바람으로
풀잎 바스락바스락
가지는 속살속살
큰 줄기는 쑥설쑥설로
음률적 예술에 심취된 나의 감상성感傷性

가을엔
맑은 물이
바위틈에 종알종알
골짜기에 중얼중얼
시냇가에 쫑알쫑알
음성의 묵상에 잠기는 나의 다정다감

가을엔
공허한 벌판에
마음이 앞서는 반향의 선율 따라
노을 속 갈매기와 들새 떼 끼리끼리

92

Autumn

In the soft wind of autumn,
   Rustling passing the grass leaves,
Whispering passing the thin branches
   And talking in a subdued tone
Passing the large stems,
   I'm a sentimentalist to be attracted
With the rhythmic arts.

In the clear water of autumn,
   In grumbles of a gap, in mutters of the valley
And in murmurs of the brook.
   I'm a visual and auditory sense to resign myself
To silent meditation of voice.

In an empty of autumn,
   The gulls and wild birds of a feather flock together
In the sunset in accordance with the melody
   Of the echo before my mind.

깨끗한 밤하늘에 외로운 별들의 윙크는
고독을 음미하여 심오한 사상을 깨닫게 하려는 듯
향수에 젖는 산자락 물드는 모습의 수채화를
그려두고 싶어라.

The winks of lonely stars in the clear night sky
    Seem to try to understand the profound thought
By enjoying loneliness.
    I want to paint well in watercolors of the mountain
To be wetted by nostalgia.

95

가을이 가는 소리

창창한 잎들의 자긍심 접고
맑은 햇빛에 반짝반짝 물들어
안으론 체념
밖으론 선연嬋娟한 얼굴 활짝 핀 채
가을이 가는 익살떠는 소리

날개 펴 허공으로 이륙하는 기러기 떼
V자 편대나 종횡을 유지하기도 하면서
지난 번뇌를 털어버리려는 듯

밤마다
가깝게 멀리 들려오는
낙엽의 홀가분한 소리와 함께
쓸쓸한 풀벌레의 하모니

가을은
지루한 녹색 셈을 끝내고
황금빛 생명력의 소망으로
장중한 정신력의 고동소리만.

The Sounds of Autumn

Folding the self-praise of deep blue leaves
    And being stained glitteringly in clear sunlight,
Autumn is an antic sounds,
    As it's resigned inside
And gloomed with a beautiful face on the outside.

A flock of geese spread their wings
    And take off into the air.
While maintaining the V-shaped formation
    and vertically and horizontally,
It seems that it's going to shake off the last agony.

The harmonies of the lonely grass insects spread
    With the sounds of the hollows
Of the fallen leaves coming close and far away
    To each other at night.

Fall has just finished the tedious green counts
    And seemed to have only told the heartbeats
Of solemn mental power
    Through the long-cherished desire
Of golden vitality.

가을 하늘 아래

드높고 푸른 하늘 아래
물결이 보이는 언덕에 서면
지상으로 사뿐히 치솟다
안착하는 갈매기 떼처럼
내 마음은 홀가분한 두근거림

금빛 햇살 수면에 키스하고
맑은 하늘 아래
고추잠자리 떼 지어 날고
나뭇가지들 반나체와
길가 코스모스는
날씬한 몸매로 춤 솜씨 뽐내며
황금물결 곡식들은
보기만 해도 풍성해지는 이 마음

쌀쌀한 바람결에 심중에 회상한즉
젊은 날 힘겨운 멍에를 하나 둘씩 벗어
"공수래공수거"의 진리 앞에
나의 헛된 생각은 옅은 안개 같은 구름.

98

Under the Autumn Sky

Standing on a hill to be overlooked the waves
  Under a high and blue autumn sky,
My heart throb at the sight
  Like a swarm of seagulls soaring
And sitting softly on the ground.

The golden sunshine kisses the waves,
  A group of white clouds drifting
In high clear sky fly away,
  The red dragonflies take wing in a flock
Under them and the semi-nudes of branches
  And cosmoses by the roadside
Boast a dancing skills with their slender bodies.
  It's my mind that becomes rich
Even if I see the grain of golden waves.

Recalling to my heart in the chilly wind
  And casting off one and two of the hard yoke
On my young day,
  My meaningless thoughts are clouds with hazy fog
Before the truth of "Come empty, Return empty."

가을 흥취

사붓사붓 밟노라면
가을이 영그는 울림 속
눈길 닿는 곳마다
황홀하게 채색彩色되는 풍경화

황금빛 산야에
열매는 종류와 색상대로
사과와 감은 핑크색 공
머루와 포도는 흑색 얼굴
무와 당근은 흙속에서 몸 자랑
그것들은 건강에 도움을 주는 감칠맛

풍성한 계절과 함께
부푼 꿈을 통해
국화처럼 소슬한 노스탤지어가 솟아올라
순결무구純潔無垢한 미망인의 외로움 바라본 듯
대자연의 섭리 앞에
흐뭇해지는 코러스에 흥취.

Fall Interests

If I tread the plain with soft steps
    That the sun spreads its beams,
It's the landscape painting to be colored absorbedly
    Within my eye-shot in the echo
That the fall fruits corn.

According to their fruitful kinds and colors
    In the golden fields and mountains,
Apple and persimmon are pink balls,
    Wild vine and grape are black faces,
Radish and carrot are proud of their bodies
    In the earth.
Those are crunchy taste of them
    To help our health.

With the abundant season,
    It seems to have looked at the loneliness
Of a chastity widow for me to spring
    A chilly nostalgia like a chrysanthemum
Through the swing dreams.
    I'm interested to the chorus which is filled
With providence of Mother Nature.

101

고향 그리워

담양과 순창을 잇는 금성산 기슭
숲 사이 윙크하는 그 빛 따라
병정놀이 헤엄치던 그 자리엔
새들과 잎들의 노래가 울려 퍼지는 듯

지난 희미한 기억 속
야생화와 풀냄새 연상하니
노란 잎도 한때는 초록인데
지금 내 곁은
부질없는 단풍 같은 생각으로
가슴 찢는 간사한 마음만 야울야울

내 고향 산천초목 그대로인데
구름 가듯
강물 흐르듯
산 넘고
물 건너
아파트 숲길 내딛는 실향의 망향 안고
숙연한 노을을 바라보는 노년의 추상화를 구상.

A Nostalgic Hometown

Along the winking light between the forests
   At the foot of the mountains,
Connecting Damyang and Sunchang,
   It seems that the songs of the birds and leaves
Are heard in the place where I swam
   With playing soldiers.

Being reminiscent of the wild flower and grass smell
   In the last faint memory,
Even though the yellow leaves were green at one time,
   Now my side is maple-like thoughts
With the uselessness and only a cunning heart
   That tears my heart.

My mountain vegetation of hometown is just as it is,
   Flying like a cloud, flowing like a river,
Going o'er the mountains and crossing the water.
   Holding my homesickness sentiment to take
The apartment forest path, I think the abstract picture
   Of old age to look at a reverential glow.

103

구름의 방랑

푸른 하늘 지붕 삼고
서로서로 포옹하여
헤어질 줄 모르는 인연
바람의 칼춤에
한 양떼들처럼 제 갈 길

백의 천사로 자유로 즐기다
지쳐 버린 먹구름
못다 이룬 사연에
생사간의 엄숙한 퍼즐
푸념하듯 눈물 쏟는 몸부림

한 조각 바람이나 새같이
대륙과 바다 사이
무비자로 횡단
고향을 등진 채
슈베르트의 "방랑자"* 멜로디처럼
푸른 하늘 흐늘흐늘.

*원명 : 방랑자
*작곡 : 슈베르트(독일, 1816)
*내용 : 19세 소년의 작품으로 피로한
  방랑자의 행복과 절망의 가곡.

104

The Wanderer of Clouds

The clouds take the blue sky as a roof
  And are an endless relationship to hug
One another.
  However, they go each on their way
Like a flock of sheep with a sword dance
  Of them.

Enjoying freely as a white angel,
  The tired clouds are a struggle to pour tears
As if to complain about the solemn puzzles
  Between life and death
In the story not to be made.

Like a wind or a bird,
  They cross between the continent and sea
Without a visa.
  Being on bad terms with their hometown,
They hover o'er the blue sky
  Like a Schubert's "Wanderer" * melody.

*Source : Der Wanderer
*Composition : Franz P. Schubert(Germ. 1816)
*Contents : It's a song of the happiness and despair
  of the tired wanderer of 19 years old work.

국화꽃 단상

지친 초록 노랗게 물든
소박미素朴美 넘치는
비상飛上하는 꿈의 숨결

수정 같은 이슬과
청초한 서릿발의 만남으로
이 세상을 현혹시키면
사람들 흥에 겨워 히히거리고
은은한 향에
쌓인 울분을 태우는
깊은 혼의 등불

그 탐스러운 송이에 울렁울렁
늙어가는 생각 잠시 잊고
황금빛에 허공의 침묵을 움켜잡아
내 영혼의 영원한 안식의 심호흡.

106

Chrysanthemum Fragmentary

The tired green has changed to yellow.
  It seems to feel the breath of flying dream
Overflowing with naive beauty.

When they dazzle the world with meeting
  Of crystal dew and neatly frost columns,
People are hurting in the excess of mirth.
  They're a lamp of a deep soul to burn up
The suppressed grief
  Owing to the subtle perfume.

My heart beats quick at the desirable blossoms.
  I forget the thinking of growing old
For a moment.
  And then I grab the silence of the air
In the golden light
  And divert my deep breath
Of the eternal rest of my soul.

추락하는 나뭇잎 보니

긴 여름에 지친 몸
가을 되어 홀가분하게
자유를 만끽하지만
외로움과 숙연함을 몸소 실천하는
시간의 힘에 떠밀려가는 빈손 자세

정열의 녹색 꿈 어디를 가고
아쉬운 추억의 무게를
바람의 날개에 실린 채
햇빛 달빛이
다음 기약의 여운을 남기우고

그들은 정해진 길이 없는데도
그놈의 명령대로
숨 가쁘게 순종하여
골짜기 늪 편한 곳에 거하는데

난
속세의 아픈 마음 달래
번뇌에 찬 무거운 발길은
어디에 어떻게 고이 머물고.

Seeing the falling Leaves

Being tired body in the long summer
　　And enjoying freedom fully
With being lightly dressed in fall,
　　But they're the empty-handed posture
To be pushed by the power of time to practice
　　Loneliness and solemn personally.

The green dream of passion where it is,
　　As the weight of unsatisfied feelings
And memories is carried on the wings of the wind.
　　The sunlight and the moonlight
Seem to linger for the next promise.

Even though they have no fixed way,
　　They obey its commands for lack of breath
And have taken a good rest in the valleys
　　Or swamps.

I'm relieved of my sad mind of world
　　And I wonder where and how I stay nicely
For my heavy steps of anguish.

109

5

겨울 나뭇가지

Winter Twigs

겨울 나뭇가지

뿌리의 입술 자양분 빨아
빛과 바람에 연합
벼랑 끝에 맑은 영혼의 날개
허공의 추위와 어우르면서
인고의 억센 침묵의 낭만적 율동은
모두 버리겠다는 내 마음까지도
달래려 하고

눈보라에 알몸 샤워
깨끗한 영혼을 단련하는 순교자처럼
기도의 손길은
죄 없이 산다는 증표로
언제나 제자리 지키는 강한 의지

여름날 열정은
식은 미련으로 남아
보이지도 들리지도 않는 맥박 속
쓰라린 고통을 망각한 채
한을 삭이는 일편단심에
난 부끄러워 가슴이 철렁.

112

Winter Twigs

Sucking the nourishment with the lips of the roots
    Uniting together in the light and wind,
The wings of a clear soul on the edge of the cliff
    Join with the cold in the air.
The romantic rhythms of strong silence of endurance
    Try to divert my mind to abandon everything.

Even if they shower naked in a snowstorm
    Like martyrs who train up clean souls,
Their hands of prayer are the strong will
    That always keeps its place
Owing to a token of innocence.

The summer passions remained faded.
    Forgetting the nasty pains
In the invisible and inaudible pulses,
    I'm ashamed and heartbroken
Through the passionate devotion
    To appease their bitter feelings.

113

겨울 날 단상

지난 날 무지개 맵시
지금은 회색에
뼛속까지 시려
덧없는 겨울동안
어디론가 서서히 죽어가는 신세

차갑게 스미는 몸에
심장의 고동은 희미해져
흰 드레스 느낌으로
바람과 춤을

피할 수 없는 생의 겨울
그리움이 치솟는
가슴의 들판에
마냥 즐거웠던 그 시절의
녹색 즐거움 회상하니
맑은 영혼의 이상화가 그리워져
하얀 꽃잎들의 양탄자를

114

혼자만이 맨 먼저 밟고 싶은 걸.

Fragmentary of Winter Day

The good figures of past rainbow
　Are now ashy-pale
And chill me to the bone.
　They're slowly dying circumstances
Anywhere during the fleeting winter.

As the heartbeats of my body to be coldly infused
　Grow dim with age,
I dance with the wind in a white dress feeling.

In the field of my soaring breast
　Through the winter of unforgettable life,
Looking back upon the green pleasures
　To be always enjoyed,
I'm yearned for the idealization of a clear soul.
　I want to step on the carpet of white petals alone
Before everything else.

겨울 산 오르면

눈 내리는 산 오르면
포근한 정경의 심연 속
세속잡사 생각은
바위 틈새 솔향과
홀가분한 자유의 설운으로
산언덕을 쓸어가고

눈이 펑펑 내리는 산 오르면
설경의 깨끗함 속
마음 비우는 방법이 익혀져
심중에 영감이 솟아
민첩한 눈동자는
눈 쌓인 경치와 하나 되며

신선한 공기를 벗으로 산 올라
숲속 흰 눈송이와 어울리니
덧없이 사라져가는 추억들
내 얼굴에 스치는 듯
자연과 나의 일체감 속
마냥 흐뭇한 것을.

116

Climbing up Winter Mountain

If I climb up the mountain of falling snow,
   The thought of secular affairs
In the abyss of comfortable sight sweeps away
   The mountain cliffs in the pine fragrance
Of rocky crevices and snow and cloud
   Of light freedom.

When I climb up the mountain
   Where the snow falls heavily,
I'm well aware of the way of emptying my mind
   And inspire from my heart in the cleanliness
Of the snow scene.
   My agile pupils become one with snowy scenery.

Climbing up the mountain with the friends
   Of fresh air
And running with white snowflakes In the woods,
   I'm joyful of nature and my sense of unity
As if the memories disappearing suddenly
   Touch my face.

겨울 향수

하얀 눈길 따라
무거운 발걸음 멈추고
영의 서치라이트 켜면
흰나비 떼 나의 눈을 즐겁게 하고

그 가벼운 깃털
꽃잎같이 흩날리다
지친 몸 지상에 키스하면
개성은 어디로 날고
희로애락은 헛되게 감돌아
한운야학閒雲野鶴이 마음 속 무료함을 달래

냉기의 대기권에
생장과 소멸의 윤회로
회한의 눈물을 삭히며
은혜의 설풍 따라
상처 난 영혼의 시린 뼛속이
시원하게 가벼워지는 날까지 위무慰撫의 감화로
겨울 향수의 단맛 쓴맛을 다 보았으면.

118

Winter Nostalgia

The flocks of white butterflies amuse my eyes
    For me to stop my heavy steps
And turn on the searchlight of my soul
    Along the white snow road.

When the light feathers scatter like petals
    And tired bodies kiss the ground,
Their personalities flee somewhere
    And joy and anger go round in vain.
The carefree life relieves tedium of my heart.

They digest the tears of remorse
    With the cycles of growth and extinction
In the atmosphere of freezing.
    I want to taste the sweets and bitters
Of winter nostalgia with the good influence
    Of pacification until the chilled bone insides
Of wounded soul become cool and light
    Through wind blowing through the snow of grace.

겨울 호숫가를 거닐면

사뿐히 눈 내리는 호숫가를 거닐면
가슴이 울렁울렁
한세상 바라는 뜻 묵상하면
마냥 홀로 걷고 싶은 충동을

시린 눈 지그시 감으면
고요하게 쌓이는 소리로
추억 속 졸리는 상
자연의 숨결로 돌아와
몸부림치다 지쳐버린 듯

지금에 와서
누구를 애타게 기다린다거나
낭만적 사연도 없이
허탈감에 마음의 거울만 바라볼 뿐

얼어붙은 호숫가를 거닐면
지난 싱그럽고 활발했던 패기는
무거운 침묵 속 하얗게 엎드린 채
알몸으로 벙어리 냉가슴인 것을.

Taking a Stroll on the Lakeside in Winter

Walking through the snow-covered lakeside,
　　I throb with tossing and leaping.
Graving the desire for my life time,
　　I'm urged by impulse to walk alone.

As I close my chill eyes,
　　It seems to have been tired of struggling
For all the things to be fallen asleep in memories
　　With the sounds piled up of the silent movements
To return to the breath of nature.

In hindsight,
　　I wait for someone or don't have a romantic story,
I only look at the mirror of my mind
　　In state of collapse.

Walking across a frozen lakeside,
　　I suffer in silence with nothing on
As the last lively and ambitious spirits
　　Have fallen asleep in white
Through the heavy silence.

121

나목이여

눈보라 날리는 쓸쓸한 광야에
공허만이 감도는 태초의 환상곡을 듣는 듯
앙상한 가지들 떨면서도
위풍늠름에 빈손운동 즐기는 나목이여

발가벗은 수치를 망각한 채
가지마다 성애性愛의 서걱 소리
깡그리 야윈 몸 하늘 우러러
고행자苦行者의 숨결로
뼈를 깎는 아픔을 기다림으로
인내하는 보람찬 삶이어라

처량한 자기완성의 순명殉名의 길에
부동자세의 보초병처럼
자화상 하나 크게 남기려는
자연의 순리에 순종하며
봄의 부활을 담금질하는 그리움 안고
네 몸에 흐르는 교만의 차림새를 벗어 던지며
허전한 양심의 창고를 채우는
낮은 자세의 가슴인 나목이어라.

122

Nude Trees

In a desolate wilderness where a snowstorm blows,
   I seem to hear the fantasia in the beginning
In which only the void can be felt.
   It's a nude tree which enjoys free gymnastics
Majestically, trembling with their thin branches.

Forgetting the naked shame,
   Groaning with the crunch as munching at an apple
And looking up to the heaven with their thin bodies,
   They find their life worth living to be patient
By waiting for the pain of cutting off the bones
   Like the ascetics's breath.

They're obedient to nature's reasonableness
   In order to leave a self-portrait bigger
Like an immobile posture in the way of dying for a fame
   Of their pitiable self-fulfillment
And nude trees with a low stance chest
   For the sake of filling the storehouse
Of an empty conscience,
   Throwing off the proud attires of their body
With the longing to quench spring's rebirth.

눈 내리는 속을

하얗게
빈 마음으로 날갯짓
순결의 춤가락이 너무 고와
더러운 것일랑 모두 순백으로
오만의 태도를 취하지 못한 채

천지간 자유의 몸으로
추한 사연들 휘저으며
깨끗하고 아름답게
쌓인 훈훈한 선물은
시린 영혼을 포근히 위로하고

은혜의 희생적 눈물 되어
부끄럽고 더러운 흔적 지우는
신비로움의 공명共鳴으로
호연지기 터전에 연주되는
장엄한 심포니를 감상함이라.

124

Through the falling Snow

The snowflakes fly a flap of the wings
    With empty hearts in white.
Their pure dancing is so good.
    All of the dirty things are white
And can't take the attitude of arrogance.

They disturb the ugly stories
    With the free bodies
Twixt sphere and glebe.
    The nice and warm gifts wrapped
Cleanly and beautifully comfort the chill spirit.

Being the resonance of the mystery of trying
    To cover up the shameful and dirty traces
Of sacrificial tears of grace,
    I appreciate a magnificent symphony
That is played on the base of vast-flowing spirit.

설편雪片의 일생

발랄한 유희로
상하
좌우로
자유경쟁 속
생명을 지키려는 온몸의 흐느낌

염치없는 취설吹雪과 함께
쓸쓸한 하강기류를 즐기다가
영혼의 아픈 흔적들 달래
멀리 가까이 사라진 흰 꽃잎들

하늘나라 눈사태 떠나
지상의 아귀다툼 아우성에
후회의 괴로움을 삭이는 듯
그 영적 꿈의 서정은
온갖 추한 것 묻어 버린 이매지
나에겐
세월을 낚는 바람과 함께
서글픈 무아애.

126

The Life of a Snow

Through lively play,
  They're the whole body's sobs
To protect their lives
  In free competition
Of up and down and side to side.

Enjoying the descent airflow of lonesomeness
  With a shameless blizzard,
They're white petals vanished far away
  From the painful traces of their soul.

They've come far and far from the avalanche
  Of the kingdom of heaven
And seem to digest the bitterness of regret
  In the outcry of quarrel.
I'm a sad selfless love with the wind
  To catch the years through the image
For the lyric of spiritual dream
  To bury all the ugliness.

설화雪花를 바라보니

눈 내리는 잿빛 하늘 바라보니
안개구름 속을 탈출하는
순결무구純潔無垢의 흰 나비 떼
거침없는 춤사위
내 영혼의 동반자

흰 눈 바라보니
천사들 드레스 날개는
천상 비밀을 몸짓의 언어로
보고 듣게 하려는 듯

멀리 쌓인 솜이불 바라보니
산들은 깊은 생각에 잠긴 정숙한 신부
나무들은 맨몸으로 추위를 망각한 채
앙상한 가지에 눈부시게 피어난
환희의 분분설에
내 생각은
영혼의 메아리와 어울리는 물심일여物心一如.

128

Looking at Snowflakes

Looking at the gray sky with the snow falling,
  I see a flock of white butterflies to escape
Through the stratus.
  Showing flowing dancing skills,
They're the companions of my soul.

Looking at white snowflakes,
  The angel's dress wings try to see and hear
Through the language of gestures in heaven's secrets.

When I look at the cotton comforter piled up
  In the distance,
The mountains are silent brides in deep thought.
  As the trees obliterate the cold
With their naked bodies,
  I'm unity of matter and spirit that mingles
With the echo of my soul in the snowflakes of joy
  To be dazzled on the sparse branches.

함박눈이 펑펑 내려

함박눈이 펄펄 내리다
날갯짓 멈추면
산야와 빌딩은 은혜의 품에
순백의 정신으로 소복소복

함박눈이 펑펑 내리다
춤동작 멈추면
추한 세상 사라지고
깨끗한 마음이 새록새록

함박눈이 갈팡질팡 내리다
자유스러움이 멈추면
충동적 생각은 평온으로
참 하늘의 뜻 살랑살랑

함박눈이 훨훨 내리다
닿는 곳 멈추면
쌓인 곳의 경치는
설풍의 설렘과 함께
메아리 들리는 듯 하롱하롱.

Snow is coming down in large Flakes

When the snowflakes begin to flutter in the air
    and stop their wing-beats,
All the things on the ground are stacked
    In the spirit of pure white in the bosom of grace.

When they begin to fall thick in a flap
    And stop their dancing,
The ugly world goes out of sight
    And a clean heart arises in succession.

When they begin to fall in a flap
    And stop their freedoms,
Their impulsive thoughts are transformed
    Into calmness
And rustled in the meaning of the true heaven.

When they begin to fall briskly
    And stop where they reach,
The sight of snow-covered place
    Seems to be heard echoing
With the wind blowing through the snow.

131

6

❧

나에게 주려는 선물
A Gift meant for me

나에게 주려는 선물

바람과 물 함께하니
희고 푸른 스윙의 원무곡圓舞曲에
가물가물 웃음꽃은
창조자의 솜씨로
수평선상에 종합예술로 위로하고

곡선미 휘감기는 비탈진 자락에
들끓는 영적 메아리는
포말로 사라지면서까지
넘치는 정열을 본받으라는 것 같아

일정한 몸매나 얼굴도 없이
왔다가는 아무런 미련이 없는데도
나 같은 자들의 혼과 영을
쪼개기까지 하는 묵시默示로
인류사회에 봉사하는 전환점을 생각하라는 듯.

134

A Gift meant for Me

The wind and the water are joined together,
    All the flickering smiles in the distance
In the white and blue swing waltz are bloomed
    As a synthetic art on the horizon
By the creator's skill.

The spiritual echo to be excited
    Into the slanting hem entwined with curve
Seems to be full of sigh and passion
    Until disappearing into a foam.

Even though there's no constant body and face
    And no lingering attachment to come and go,
It is an apocalypse that even divides the souls
    And spirits of people like me
And seems to think of a turning point
    To serve human society.

135

나팔수喇叭手

바다 몸 속 해독 위해
하얀 피 토하면서까지
온 힘을 다하는 바다의 열정에
새 아침 새 물결 나팔수

점점 더 병든 바다의 찌푸린 이맛살 얼굴
하늘 향해
하얀 이빨 보여
사자처럼 달려오는 몸짓에
황금빛 입술 나팔수

겉으론 미소
속으론 찡그림이
왈츠리듬에 알몸의 경련을 일으키면서까지
온 세상 정수淨水를 바래
난 동심의 기둥에 기대어
혼자만의 용서와 화해를 구하는데
눈물로 호소하는 포말 나팔수.

136

Trumpeter

I see the new wave trumpeter
  On the morning in the passion of the sea
To do all the hard work until pouring the white blood
  For the detoxification in the body of sea.

It's the lips trumpeter of gold in a gesture
  That rushes like a lion
For the knitted brows of countless faces
  Of an increasingly bad sea
To show the white teeth towards the sphere.

The smiles on the outside
  And the frown in the inside is to be desirous
Of the clean water of the whole world
  Until torturing to the naked spasm
In the waltz rhythm.
  It's the foam trumpeter that comforts with tears
For me to lean on the pillars of child's mind
  For a moment and seek lonely forgiveness
And reconciliation.

137

물결은

물결은
하얗게
푸르게
수평 위 수증기로 날다가
자유로운 구름의 신세로 멈추면
비가 되고

증기의 입자가 햇빛을 받으면
수평선 뛰어넘어
반원형 홍교虹橋라

삶도 죽음도 아닌 공간에 떠돌다
수평면에 머물면
거대한 바다가 되어
모든 것 포용하여 정화시키려 하여

이 내 몸 한숨은 눈물이 되어
해도 달도 없는 먼 길 배회하다
서글픈 마음의 물결로
모래나 바위에 부딪쳐
흰 구슬로 포말일세.

Waves

The waves are white and blue
  And they pass off in vapor above the horizon.
Stopping by free clouds, they will rain.

When the particles of water vapor are exposed
  To the sunlight,
They make a semicircular rainbow
  O'er the horizon.

Wandering through a space
  That is neither life nor death
And staying on a horizontal plane,
  They become a huge sea
And try to purify everything by embracing it.

The sigh of my body becomes a tear
  And wanders a long way without sun and moon,
And it's only a foam with the white pearls to be hit
  A sand or a rock with a wave of sadness.

139

바람과 파도

부드러우면서도
때로는 야멸찬 심통의 함성 속
대자연의 대합창을 시청하노라면
바다 건너 그리움을 쌓더니
영영 그 파도의 가슴앓이가
내 마음에 메아리쳐

바람의 의지대로
부서지고 비벼대다 다시 연합
서로 어색한 웃음을 망각한 채
정직한 세월 앞에 교제를 잉태하여
제 각기 길로 추스르는 마음들

밀물과 썰물이 교차하는 해변엔
평화 노래의 향연이 일어
그대의 넓은 마음같이 되고 싶지만
약하고 노도 같은 면도 보여
난 매순간을 바다에서
뗏목 타는 심정으로 살고파.

140

Wind and Waves

Seeing and hearing of a grand chorus in the rhythm
    Of Mother Nature through softness
And sometimes shouting of cold disposition,
    I've got a long across the sea.
But the heartbreak of the waves for good echoes
    In my heart.

Only the will of the wind is rubbed and broken,
    And then united.
Forgetting each other's forced laughing,
    They're conceived an acquaintance
Before the honest time.
    Each of them is naked without a bone to manage
To his own way.

A feast was laid in the song of peace on the beach
    Of tide and ebb. I want to look like your wide mind.
But, being weak and in that angry waves,
    I'm going to live every moment like a sailboat ride
On the sea.

141

수평선을 바라보면

수평선상에
둘이 하나로 보여
흔들리는 몸짓은
내 마음을 흔들어놓아
진정될 수 없는 열망의 형상形象

하늘과 물결 사이
곡선과 굴곡이 공존하는
동양화와 서양화의 하모니
비바람에 씻기어도
자연의 원소는 살아남아
그 무엇으로도 밀어낼 수 없는
신루蜃樓의 추억追憶

낮과 밤
바람과 물결 연주는
방향의 감각을 망각한 채
영원에서 순간으로
보일 듯 사라질 듯
그 신묘한 교향에 기상奇想.

142

Seeing the Horizon

The two seem to be one on the horizon.
  A shaking gesture is a form of aspiration
That can't suppress myself
  By swaying my heart.

There's a harmony of oriental paintings
  And western paintings
In which curves and indentations coexist
  Between the sky and the waves.
Nature's elements survive
  Even if those are washed in wind and rain.
They're are memories of a mirage
  Not to be pushed out by anything.

Forgetting the sense of direction by playing
  On the wind and waters
Through the day and night,
  They seem to be seeing and disappearing
From eternity to moment
  And are a fantastic idea
In the wonderful symphony.

143

어머님의 등은

어머님의 손은
논밭 김매기 후
도랑에서 등 물붓기와 거친 손으로 닦아
피곤을 치유하는 약손의 추억

어머님의 등은
강풍과 눈보라에도
헌신적 노력과 애태우면서까지
방어선防禦線에 추억의 로맨틱한 사연
하지만 지금엔
어머님 지칠 때까지
업힐 수 없는 어린 시절의
체념할 수 없는 러브스토리

어머님의 등은
하늘나라에서 무시로
녹슨 내 영혼 노크하여
온갖 지혜를 준 듯
내 가슴에 멍든 훈패勳牌의 꽃
곱게 피어나도록
피눈물로 기도하는 추억의 자장가로
영원한 애정의 요람인 것을.

My Mother's Back

Her hands are a cradle of memory
   Of her medicinal hands that heal my tiredness,
Pouring the ditch water my back and washing it
   With her rough hands after weeding the fields.

Even in strong winds and snowstorms,
   Her back is a romantic story
Of the defensive line
   Until making her dedicated efforts And worrying herself.
But now, it's an inconsolable love story
   Of my childhood that can't be taken on her back
Until she is tired out.

She seems to knock my rusty soul at any time
   And give me all the wisdom in heaven.
It is the cradle of eternal affection
   As a melody of lullaby to pray with tears of blood
So that the flower of my wounded decoration
   In my heart may bloom beautifully

열심히 살 뿐

바람 따라 구름 타고
연화年華의 채찍질에
이마엔 주름살 물결
그 위엔 백발의 깃발

젊음엔 울렁이는 기쁨의 감동
때로는 가슴에
슬픈 사연도 일지만
그 갈등의 눈물은
체념의 용단이 큰 힘

살아온 길 되돌아보니
추억은 묵묵한 청산이고
잔잔한 파도라
지금까지의 내 몸때
씻고 흘러 보내
과거를 지혜의 거울삼아
이 순간을 열심히 살 뿐.

146

Living Hard

Riding in the clouds along the wind,
    The wave of wrinkles is on the forehead
And the flags of white hairs flap on it
    On the whip of time and tide.

There's a deep emotion of joy
    And a sad story may remain in the chest in youth.
But the tears of conflict are only a power
    With the decisive resolution of resignation.

Looking back on my life,
    My memories are a green mountain of silence
And calm waves.
    Washing my body's dirt until now and flowing away,
I'm going to consider my past as a mirror of wisdom
    And live this moment with zeal.

147

자유자재의 나비

살랑살랑 바람결에
땀 한 방울 보이지 않은 채
자재를 만끽한 곡예비행

꽃나무와 송이 사이
설레는 가슴 안고
날렵한 몸부림은
부러움에 극도의 운치

여기저기 꽃을
살금살금 무례하게 숨박질로
꽃에서 꽃으로 넘나드는
공존동생의 삶

현란한 옷차림에
숨 막힐 듯 춤가락 보이다
지친 날개 접고 사뿐사뿐 착륙하면
순미한 입술로 꿈을 도둑질하는
신묘한 살기다툼.

148

Butterflies of Perfect Freedom

It's an acrobatic flight that enjoys freedom
   Without showing a drop of sweat
In a rustling wind.

The smart writhes with a leap of the heart
   Twixt the flowering trees and the clusters
Are the extreme elegance to envy.

They go in and out to flowers all o'er the places
   With hide-and-seek by stealth,
Showing their coexisting brother's life
   That flits from flower to flower.

149

When you show a thrilling dancing rhythm
   In gorgeous clothes
And land softly with tired wings folded,
   It looks like the wonderful survival competition
To steal dreams with lips of pure beauty.

파도를 동경함은

파도를 동경함은
넓고 깊은 늪에서
부활의 하늘 옷 입고
희원希願의 메시지를 전하는
천사의 미소를 보기 위함이고

파도를 동경함은
파도의 교향시交響詩 속
그대의 가슴이 확 열려
그 당당한 포옹과 입맞춤의 함성은
내 삶의 가슴 아픈 응어리와
슬픈 기억의 넋이 시원하게 풀리리라
유추함이며

파도를 동경함은
자연스런 만남과 교착交錯하는 이별의 인연에서
예술의 극치로
감각을 초월한 아름다운 영혼의 꿈을
영원히 사모함이라.

Longing for the Waves

My longing for the waves is to see the smile
   Of an angel,
Wearing the sky clothes of resurrection
   From the wide and deep swamps
And conveying the messages of desire.

My longing for the waves is to be analogized
   To my mind
That your heart opens wide
   In the symphonic poem of the waves
And the shout of the gracious embrace
   And kiss will refresh the heartache feeling
Of my life and soul of sad memories.

My longing for the waves is to long for
   The eternal hope of a beautiful soul
Beyond the senses
   For the lingering tones
In their natural encounters
   And the karma of separation to be complicated
To remain at the extreme of natural art.

151

파도의 숨결

당신은
바람 따라
사랑과 미움의 무법자

수정 같은 맨몸으로

Breath of the Waves

You're an outlaw of love and hatred along the wind.

You're crystal naked and bloomed to be broken
  And all wilted, and a wizard who builds
And tears down of high or low and large

꺾어지기 위해 피어졌다 시들고
고하高下와 대소의 장벽을
쌓다 헐어버리는 마법사

신출귀몰로 후대厚待와 천대를 번갈아
순간을 즐기는 곡예사

어떻게 와 어디로 가는지
오직 솔로로 광란하는
산봉우리와 협곡 사이사이
웅비하는 곡예비행사

당신의 음성은
나의 체념의 영혼을 새롭게 하는 청량제로
슈만의 "헌정獻呈"*을 완전히 감상할 줄 알게 되는
나의 모든 것.

*원명 : 헌정獻呈
*작곡 : 슈만(독일 1840)
*내용 : 애인에게 바치는 열정적 동경이 진정으로 토로됨.

Or small sizes.

You're an acrobat who enjoys the moment
  By turning to the hospitality and contempt
Through appearing in unexpected places
  And at unexpected moments.

For a wonder, how to come and where to go,
  You're an acrobatic pilot to become frantic only alone
Twixt the mountains peaks and the canyons.

Your voice is a refrigerant that refreshes the soul
  Of my resignation, and all my things
That I can fully appreciate Schumann's "dedication"*.

*Source : Widmung
*Composition : Robert Schumann(Ger. 1840)
*Contents : It's true content that speaks out a passion and a
  yearning for longing for lovers.

해안선 따라

해안 경계선
부서졌다 피어난 백목련 무리의 전진과
지쳤다 흩어지는 물보라 꽃다발로
멀어진 총 연회宴會

바다와 땅 사이
밀물과 썰물의 두 얼굴
서로 등질 수 없는
운명적 권화權化로
먼 수면의 신루蜃樓

바람의 힘 따라
해가 뜨면 수평선을 향해
영원을 사모하는 손짓의 흔들림이 있고
달이 파도의 여운 따라 뜨면
내 가슴 속 질투로부터 끓어오르는
피맺히는 숨결로 웅비雄飛.

156

Along the Coastline

Along the borderline of the coastline,
   I see the total banquet separated by the forwardness
Of the yulan crowd to be broken and to bloom
   And the bunch of the spray to be exhausted
And scattered.

Two faces of tide and ebb twixt the sea and glebe,
   It seems to be seen the mirage
Of the distant surface of water
   With the destiny incarnation that can't be estranged
Each other.

When the sun shines on the waves
   According to the wind power,
There's the shaking of the hand gesture
   To yearn for eternity towards the horizontal line.
When the moon rises along the echoes of the waves,
   It seems to be sailed through the air
With the blooming breath which bubbles up
   From jealousy in my heart.

빛과 소리는 하늘과 땅에서

브루스 크로서
미국 앤드류대학교 교수

　독자들은 김종남 7시집에 나타난 것 중에서 한국문화에 대한 충분한 통찰력을 음미하기 위해서는 한국어 마스터가 필요치 않을 것 같다. "생각만 해도"는 제목에서, 한 어머님을 한여름 밤에 비교하고 그의 언어는 주름진 옷 다리기, 오트밀 준비, 모기를 쫓기 위한 연기 피우기, 밤새 꾸벅꾸벅 졸기 그리고 헤매는 어린애를 기다리는 것이 어머님의 경험에 대한 소개이다. "어머님 등"이라는 시에서 김 시인은 논밭 김매기한 손으로 등물치기를 마음에 그리기도 하고 다른 시에서 흰 나비나 행운의 징조 그리고 한국생활에 다른 희미한 감지를 암시하기도 했다.

　그런데 김 시인의 글을 읽노라면 일본 전통적 단시를 쓰는 교과서를 읽고 아시안 시의 전통적인 형태와 김 시인의 시 구조에 일본 시 형태의 의식적(무의식적) 영향에 감명을 받았다.

158

그 예로서 "눈과 눈의 스파클"은 일본식 시의 형식을 암시하는 두 개의 친밀한 3행 스탠자로 전개되어 많은 다른 사람들처럼 명백한 시의 제목과 연결된 일련의 전통적 일본 시 형태와 같은 스탠자로 이루어지고 있다. 일본 시의 전통에서 김 시인은 자신의 주제로서 자연에 관심을 집중시키는 단순한 경향이 있지만, 드러나는 자연의 이미지에 가벼운 섬세함을 나타내기도 한다. 웃는 눈송이, 물 위 낮게 나는 외로운 야생 거위, 고기 물린 것을 암시하는 낚싯줄의 긴장, 깊은 정원에 피어나는 장미, 잎에 물 한 방울 그리고 미세한 물체에서 인간의 경험 전체를 포함하도록 잘 선택된 이미지의 재능을 실례를 들어 설명하고 있다.

분명히 3연 시의 가장 명백한 영향을 김 시인이 계절을 자주 연구한다는 것이다. "계절 따라"는 성경 전도서傳導書에 대한 명백한 암시를 통해 인간은 이 세상 빈손 들고 왔으니 또한 그같이 돌아간다는 속담의 관찰력을 표현하는 세월의 추이를 자인하기도 하고 김 시인이 인간상태를 탐구함에 얼마나 자주 계절의 순환을 향해 생각했는지, 독자는 회고적 의향을 놓칠 수 없다. 이 즐거운 계절의 시 하나를 읽는데 소요되는 시간을 독자는 잠시 흐름을 늦추고 사려 깊은 독자들은 "그 좋은 밤을 우아하게 나아가지 말라"는 딜란 토마스Dylan Thomas의 충고를 회상할 수밖에 없다.

김 시인의 많은 시들은 서울 예술 공동체인 인사동을 방문했을 때 보았던 아시아의 수수께끼 상자를 상기시켜 준다.

내부의 보물을 드러내기 위해 조심스럽게 괴롭히기 위해 고안된 이 상자들은 김 시인의 인간경험에 대한 사려 깊은 고찰은 의미 내에서 의미를 숨기는 방식으로 생각나게 한다.

예를 들면 김 시인은 "디지털 우상화"에서 현대세계기술이 창의성을 위협하고 시간을 빼앗으며 중요한 문제에서 우리를 혼란에 빠트린다는 우려를 표명하고 있다. 다른 시에서도 김 시인은 자주 꽃 이미지 —동백, 장미, 철쭉— 인간 형상의 아름다움에 멋있는 에로틱한 언어를 사용해 암시하기도 한다.

내가 한국 독자들에게 말할 수는 없지만, 영어권 독자들은 김 시인의 종종 놀랄 만한 것과 우리를 노예화시키는 "묘한 감정의 튼튼한 끈"과 독자가 한 번도 보지 못하게 하는 것처럼 보이는 "안구의 안구" 또는 벙긋거리는 눈송이의 심상心象을 반복적으로 찾아내기 위한 진가의 노력을 인정하게 될 것이다.

또한 김 시인은 "희고 파란색 번갈아치는 파도의 춤" 같이 조화하여 큰 효과를 노려 의인화를 시도하기도 했다.

숙련된 시인들은 인간 경험에 대한 그들의 언어 사용과 통찰력은 독자들을 급히 읽히게 하고 순간적으로 엘리베이터가 갑자지 멈추는 것같이 숨이 멈추게 되는 특색이 있다. 김종남 시집은 영어권 독자들에게 이 목표를 이루고 한국의 독자들도 이 경험을 공유할 것이라고 믿는다.

Light and Sound Twixt Sphere and Glebe

Dr. Bruce closser

Andrews university, U.S.A

Readers need not master Korean to appreciate the many insights into Korean culture apparent in the poems which appear in Jong-nam Kim's seventh volume, (insert title here). In a delightful poem entitled "Even though I think," Kim compares a midsummer night to a mother, and his language is an introduction to a mother's experience, ironing wrinkled clothes, preparing gruel, tending the smoke that drives away mosquitoes, nodding through the night, waiting for a sleeping child to drift away. In another poem entitled "My Mother's Back," Kim pictures a mother pouring a dish of water on her son's back and washing him with hands roughened by a day weeding in the fields. In other poems, Kim alludes to white butterflies, omens of good fortune, and other glimpses into Korean everyday

161

life.

As it happens, at the same time I was reading Kim's poems, I was also reading a textbook on writing haikus and I was struck by the conscious(or unconscious) influence of the haiku, a traditional form of Asian poetry, in the structure of Kim's poems.

"The Eyes Sparkling between You and Me," for instance, opens with two familiar three-line stanzas reminiscent of the haiku form. The poem proceeds, as do many others, in an apparent series of haiku-like stanzas linked by the poem's theme. In the tradition of the haiku, Kim frequently focuses his attention on nature as his subject matter, referring with light delicacy to simple but revealing nature images. A smiling snowflake, a solitary wild goose flying low over the water, the tension on a fishing line indicating a bite, roses blooming in a deep garden, or the single drop of water on a leaf, illustrate the capacity of a well-selected image to include the entirety of human experience in a minute object.

Clearly the most evident influence of the haiku is Kim's frequent references to seasons. "According to the Season," with its clear allusion to Ecclesiastes, acknowledges the passage of time expressing a proverbial observation that mankind comes to the world empty and returns empty. Considering how frequently Kim turns to the cycle of the seasons in his exploration of the human condition, readers cannot miss his retrospective intent. For the length of time it takes to read one of these delightful seasonal poems, the reader slows if only for a moment the passage of time. Thoughtful readers cannot help but recall Dylan Thomas's admonition, "Do not go gently into that good night."

Many of Kim's poems remind me of Asian puzzle boxes I have seen in my visits to Insadong, an artistic community in Seoul. These boxes, designed to be teased apart gently to reveal treasures inside, remind me of the way many of Kim's thoughtful reflections on human experience hide meaning within meaning. For example, in "Idolization of Digital," Kim expresses concern that the technology of our modern world threatens creativity, snatches our time, and distracts us from issues that matter. In many other poems, Kim uses frequent flower images camellias, roses, azaleas to allude in tastefully erotic language to the beauty of the human form.

163

While I cannot speak for Korean readers, English readers

will appreciate Kim's often surprising but revealing images such as "sturdy straps of odd emotions" that enslave us or "eyeballs of eyeballs" which appear to invite readers to look not once but repeatedly to find understanding, or the image of smiling snowflakes. Kim also uses anthropomorphism to great effect in lines like "the waves dance in the white and blue dress." It is a mark of skilled poets that their use of language and their insight into the human experience bring readers up short, leaving them momentarily breathless like the sudden stop of an elevator. Jong-nam Kim's volume of poetry achieves this objective for English readers, and I assume that Korean readers will share this experience.